To
DAN
and
JULIA

Reinforced binding of hardcover edition suitable for library use.

Copyright © 1990 by Ruth Heller. All rights reserved.
Published by Grosset & Dunlap, Inc.,
a member of The Putnam & Grosset Group, New York.
Published simultaneously in Canada. Sandcastle Books
and the Sandcastle logo are trademarks belonging to The Putnam & Grosset Group.
First Sandcastle books edition, 1992. Printed in Singapore.
Library of Congress Catalog Card Number: 90-80645

ISBN (hardcover) 0-448-40085-5   C D E F G H I J

ISBN (Sandcastle) 0-448-40315-3 A B C D E F G H I J

Merry-Go-Round

A Book About Nouns

Written and illustrated by
RUTH HELLER

Publishers • GROSSET & DUNLAP • New York

NOUNS
name
a person,
place or thing . . .

a **damsel**,
a **forest**,
a **dragon**,

a **king**.

These NOUNS
are all
COMMON,
and they're
very
nice,
but
PROPER
NOUNS
are
more
precise.
**King
Arthur**
is
this person.

This
place
is
Camelot.

PROPER
NOUNS
are
capitalized.

COMMON
NOUNS
are
not.

ABSTRACT
NOUNS
each
name
a
thought,
a
notion
or
emotion…

hope
and
love
and
chivalry,
courage
and
devotion,
justice,
truth
and
courtesy
and other NOUNS
we cannot see.

CONCRETE
NOUNS
can be
seen and touched,
tasted and smelled,
and heard...

persimmons
and **grapes**
and **onions**
and **pears**
and the
beautiful
song
of a
bird.

10
9
8
7
6
5
4
3
2
1

COMPOUND NOUNS
are
more
than
one
word...

countdown
is
joined
together.

Space Age
is separated...

and **merry-go-round**
is a NOUN that's
compound and…

it is hyphenated.

NOUNS are highly effective.

The last kind of NOUN is

COLLECTIVE. A **tumble** of feathers, a **clamor** of birds and a **riot** of colors abound.

NOUNS are all around.

SINGULAR NOUNS are always one – PLURALS two or more.

Just add an **S** when there's more than one…That's the way it's usually done…

daffodils and **eyes** and **ears**, **beetles**, **bows** and **roses**, **ships** and **sails** and **cabbages**, **chrysanthemums** and **noses**.

But, it isn't
always
as easy as
that.

Here come some
exceptions.
Hang onto your
hat…

and other
headdresses.

Add **es** to NOUNS ending in **s**'s, **z**'s and **ch**'s, **sh**'s and **x**'s…

albatrosses and **foxes**, **fezzes** and **boxes**, **radishes**, **squashes**, **macintoshes**, **galoshes**, **jackasses**, **eyeglasses**, **watches** and **witches**,

and more than one **ostrich** is always **ostriches**.

PLURALS
depend
on how the NOUNS end.
If
they end in a consonant
and then a **y**,
add **es** after
changing the **y**
to an **i**…
butterflies,
daisies,
pansies
and
berries,
blue-footed
boobies
and
yellow
canaries.

If a NOUN
ends in
f or **fe**

the **f** might be changed to a **v**.

Knives is the PLURAL of **knife** and **halves** is the PLURAL of **half**.

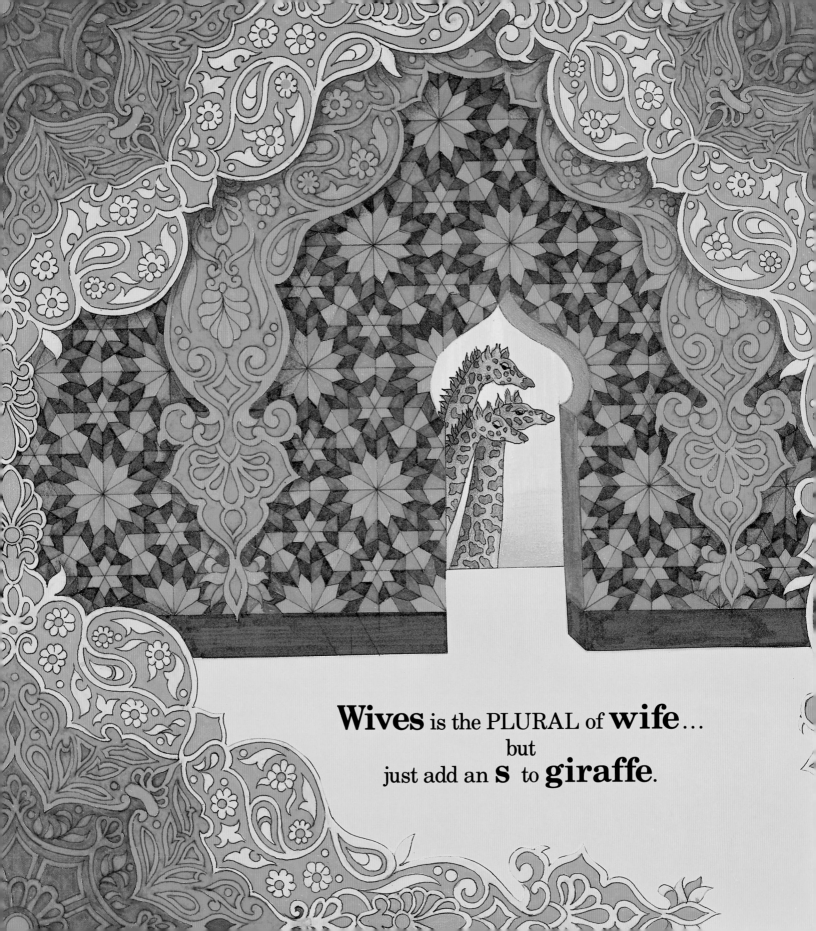

Wives is the PLURAL of **wife**…
but
just add an **s** to **giraffe**.

Which
way
should you go

when NOUNS end in **o?**

Add **es** to **tomato**
and also

potato
but…

s to **piano**
and as
to…

flamingo...
just add whichever
you wish.

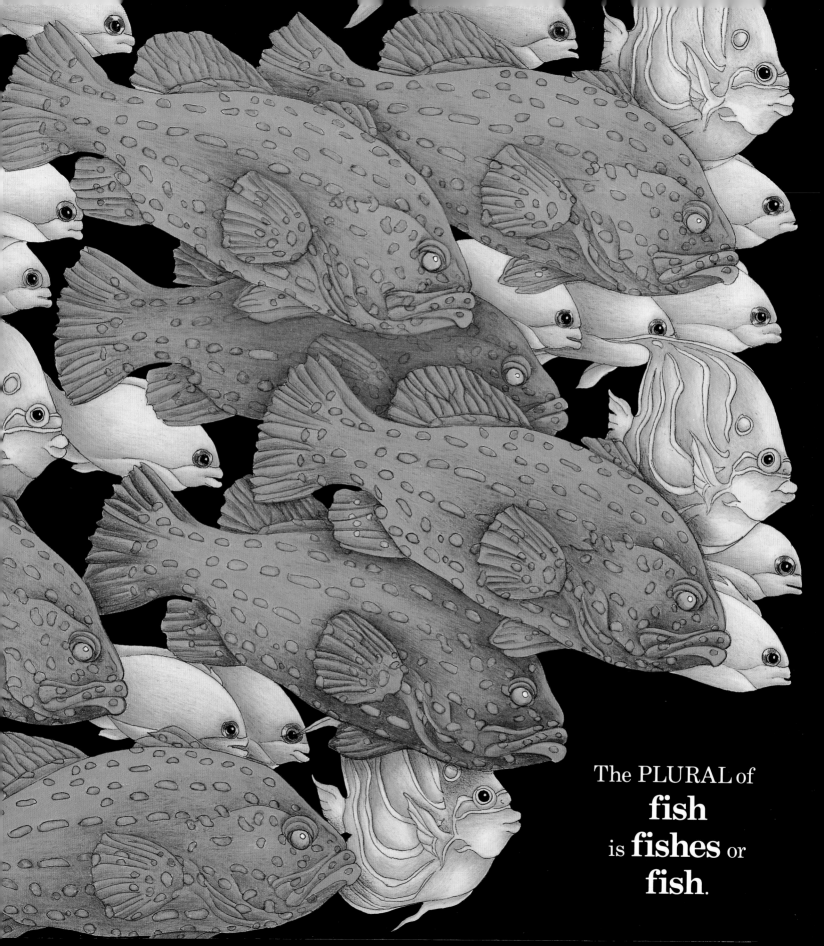

The PLURAL of
fish
is **fishes** or
fish.

Some PLURALS remain exactly the same. **Moose** is the PLURAL of **moose**.

Some change in the middle like **foot** to **feet**, and **geese** is the PLURAL of **goose**.

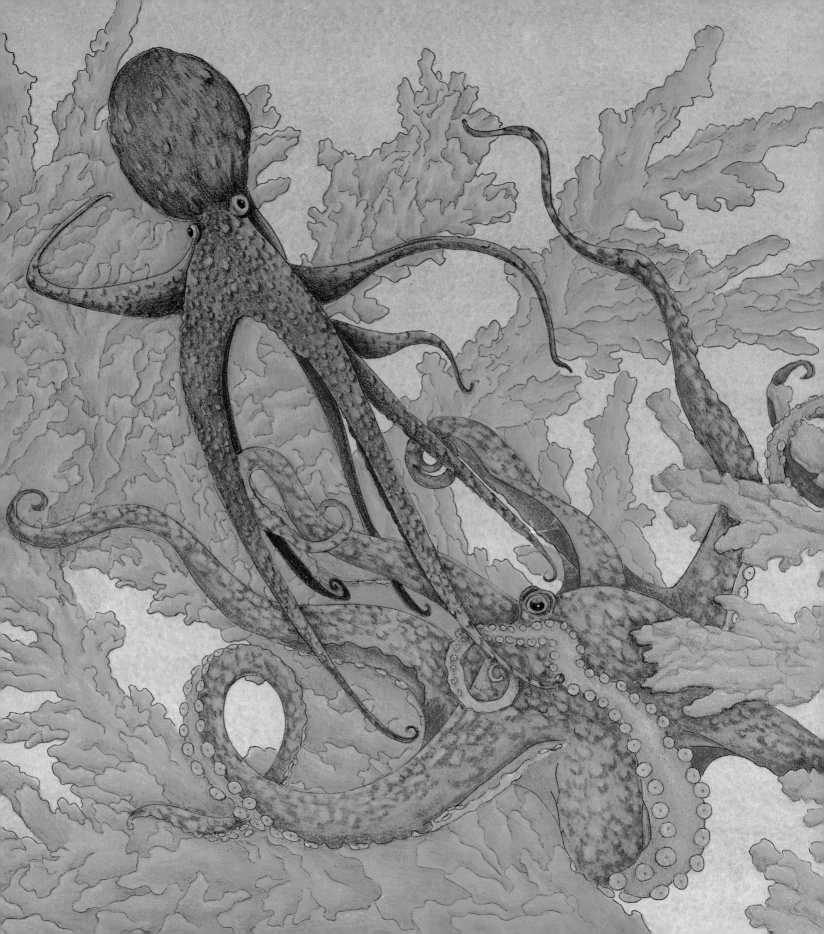

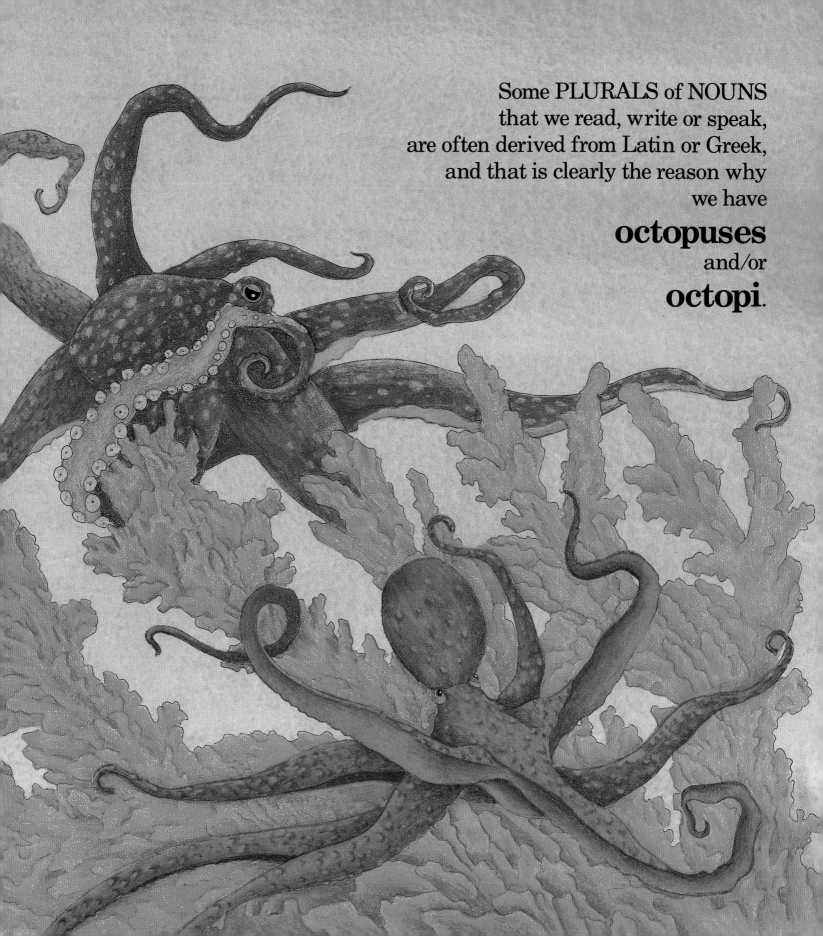

Some PLURALS of NOUNS
that we read, write or speak,
are often derived from Latin or Greek,
and that is clearly the reason why
we have

octopuses
and/or
octopi.

Now it isn't really as hard as it sounds, but be very careful of **PLURAL COMPOUNDS.**

Trunksful
and
trunkfuls are equally fine…
but the **fleur de lys** is that small French design,
and you will find, as its number increases it becomes
fleurs de lys…and not **fleur de lyses**.

Add apostrophe **S**'s
when NOUNS are POSSESSIVE,
except...

when they're PLURALS
ending in **S**'s…

the **tiger's** stripes
the **lion's** mane
the **camels'**
obvious
disdain.

NOUNS
occur
soon after
a
DETERMINER.

DETERMINERS
are numbers...
26 **cucumbers**.

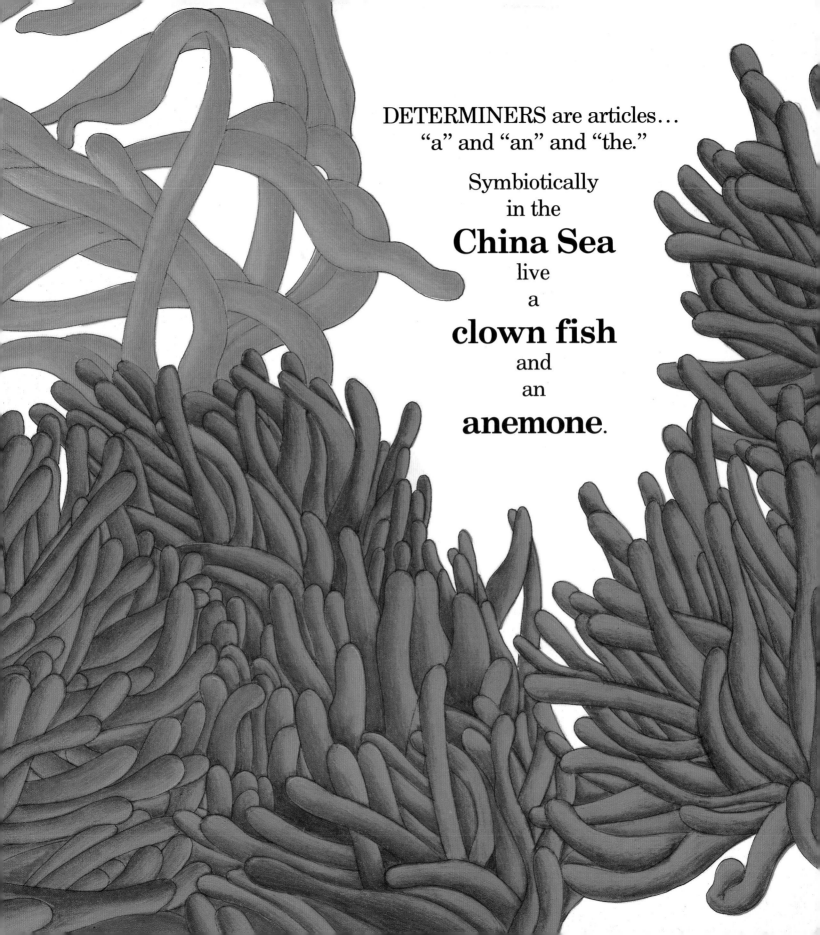

DETERMINERS are articles…
"a" and "an" and "the."

Symbiotically
in the
China Sea
live
a
clown fish
and
an
anemone.

A DETERMINER's a signal that a NOUN is on its way.

"This" is a DETERMINER....this **box**,

and so is "that"............that **fox**,

and "these" and "those"......these **hats**,

those **bows**,

and words that are indefinite...

some **daffodils**, a few **canaries**,

several **daisies**, many **berries**.

POSSESSIVES are DETERMINERS...

her **ship**, its **sail**, our **king**, his **reign**,

the tiger's **stripes**, the lion's **mane**.

DETERMINERS appear whenever NOUNS are near.

•

One last important fact...
whether COMMON or PROPER,
CONCRETE or ABSTRACT
or maybe
COMPOUND or COLLECTIVE,
each NOUN you will find
is more than one kind.

Whichever...they all are effective.

EFFECTIVE PERFORMANCE APPRAISALS: Third Edition

Robert B. Maddux

A FIFTY-MINUTE™ SERIES BOOK

CRISP PUBLICATIONS, INC.
Menlo Park, California

EFFECTIVE PERFORMANCE APPRAISALS:
Third Edition

CREDITS
Editor: **Michael G. Crisp**
Designer: **Carol Harris**
Typesetting: **Interface Studio**
Cover Design: **Carol Harris**
Artwork: **Ralph Mapson**

Copyright © 1986, 1987, 1993 by Crisp Publications, Inc.
Printed in the United States of America

Distribution to the U.S. Trade:

National Book Network, Inc.
4720 Boston Way
Lanham, MD 20706
1-800-462-6420

This book is printed on recyclable paper with soy ink.

Library of Congress Catalog Card Number 92-073962
Maddux, Robert B.
Effective Performance Appraisals
ISBN 1-56052-196-1

PREFACE

This book is for anyone who directs the activities of others. Whether a first line supervisor, the chairperson of a committee, a project leader, a school administrator, a restaurant manager, a government official, the owner of a small business, or a senior executive, you must be able to effectively discuss performance with those who report to you.

Leading a performance appraisal review can be either difficult and depressing; or dynamic and positive. The attitude, planning, and approach of the person conducting the review will make the difference.

This book will help you to think through the appraisal process, and then learn how to conduct discussions that encourage positive relationships and improved individual performances. Those who master the concepts presented will benefit from reduced stress and improved productivity.

You will have a chance to do some self-analysis which will identify personal strengths and weaknesses. Once learned, the application of the skills is up to you.

GOOD LUCK!

Robert B. Maddux

ABOUT THIS BOOK

Effective Performance Appraisals is not like most books. It stands out from other books in an important way. It's not a book to read—it's a book to *use*. The unique "self-paced" format of this book and the many worksheets encourage a reader to get involved and try some new ideas immediately.

This book will introduce the critical building blocks of how to conduct an effective performance appraisal. Using the simple yet sound techniques presented can make a dramatic change in one's productivity, accomplishments and job satisfaction.

Effective Performance Appraisals can be used effectively in a number of ways. Here are some possibilities:

—*Individual Study.* Because the book is self-instructional, all that is needed is a quiet place, some time and a pencil. By completing the activities and exercises, a reader should not only receive valuable feedback, but also practical steps for self-improvement.

—**Workshops and Seminars.** The book is ideal for assigned reading prior to a workshop or seminar. With the basics in hand, the quality of the participation will improve and more time can be spent on concept extentions and applications during the program. The book is also effective when it is distributed at the beginning of a session, so participants can "work through" the contents.

—**Remote Location Training.** Books can be sent to those not able to attend "home office" training sessions.

There are several other possibilities that depend on the objectives, program or ideas of the user. One thing's for sure, even after it has been read, this book will be looked at—and thought about—again and again.

ABOUT THE AUTHOR

Robert B. Maddux is highly regarded for his extensive experience in human resource management. In addition to his success as both a speaker and trainer, Mr. Maddux has authored several best-selling books, including *Team Building, Quality Interviewing, Successful Negotiation, Delegating for Results* and *Ethics in Business*. He is currently a Senior Vice President and Director of Professional Services for the Los Angeles Region of Right Associates.

TABLE OF CONTENTS

TABLE OF CONTENTS (continued)

I

ARE YOU READY FOR BETTER APPRAISALS?

SOME OBJECTIVES FOR YOU

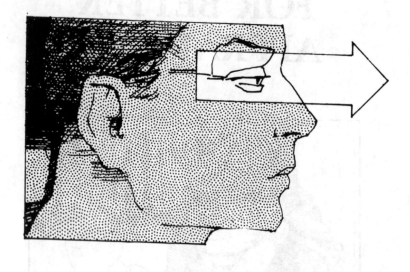

SOME OBJECTIVES FOR THE READER

> Before you begin this book, give some thought to your objectives.
>
> Objectives give us a sense of direction, a definition of what we plan to accomplish, and a feeling of fulfillment when they are achieved.
>
> Check the objectives that are important to you. Then, when you have completed the book, review your objectives and enjoy the sense of achievement you will feel.

AFTER READING AND PRACTICING THE CONCEPTS IN THIS BOOK, YOU WILL BE ABLE TO:

☐ establish a work climate conducive to productive performance appraisals;

☐ initiate and maintain positive communication about work performance versus work expectations;

☐ help your employees prepare properly for performance appraisal;

☐ prepare and conduct performance discussions that encourage an exchange of information and produce better results;

☐ follow through properly on agreements reached with the employee.

A PERFORMANCE APPRAISAL PROVIDES A PERIODIC OPPORTUNITY FOR COMMUNICATION BETWEEN THE PERSON WHO ASSIGNS THE WORK, AND THE PERSON WHO PERFORMS IT, TO DISCUSS WHAT THEY EXPECT FROM THE OTHER AND HOW WELL THOSE EXPECTATIONS ARE BEING MET.

Performance appraisals are not adversary proceedings, or social chit-chat. They are an essential communication link between two people with a common purpose.

Leading these discussions is not always easy, but the principles and techniques for effective sessions can be learned and applied by anyone.

MEET SOME SUCCESSES AND SOME FAILURES

MAKE YOUR CHOICE NOW

SUCCESSES

Leaders who engage in mutual goal setting.

Leaders who publicly recognize positive performance, and privately correct improper performance when it occurs.

Leaders who establish clear, measurable expectations, and provide a climate conducive to success.

Leaders who ask questions, listen carefully and appreciate the ideas of others.

Leaders who follow through to ensure commitments are met.

Add from your own experience:

_____

_____

_____

_____

FAILURES

Those who establish arbitrary, unilateral performance goals and/or standards.

Those who spend too much time looking for things that are wrong and too little looking for things that are right.

Those who have not thought through what they expect or don't know how to measure success. Those who provide a threatening atmosphere in which to work.

Those who never seek the ideas of others or listen, yet have a solution for everyone else's problems.

Those who do not take their own commitments seriously.

Add from your own experience:

_____

_____

_____

_____

> A good performance appraisal leaves both parties feeling they have gained something.

DO YOU TEND TO PUT OFF PERFORMANCE APPRAISALS?

Too often performance appraisals are left until the last minute and then done in a hurried manner. When this occurs, the results are poor. The supervisor feels guilty, and the employee unimportant and let down.

The facing page lists several advantages of doing thoughtful performance appraisals when they are due. Check those that are important to you.

ADVANTAGES OF DOING A GOOD JOB

WHAT A WELL-PLANNED PERFORMANCE APPRAISAL CAN DO FOR YOU

People responsible for performance appraisals often assign a low priority to them because they have not thought about the benefits of a good appraisal session. Following are some advantages of doing a professional appraisal on a timely basis. Check ✔ those that are important to you.

☐ 1. Performance appraisals give me valuable insights into the work being done and those who are doing it.

☐ 2. When I maintain good communication with others about job expectations and results, opportunities are created for new ideas and improved methods.

☐ 3. When I do a good job appraising performance, anxiety is reduced because employees know how they are doing.

☐ 4. I increase productivity when employees receive timely corrective feedback on their performance.

☐ 5. I reinforce sound work practices and encourage good performance when I publicly recognize positive contributions.

☐ 6. When I encourage two way communication with employees, goals are clarified so they can be achieved or exceeded.

☐ 7. Regular appraisal sessions remove surprises about how the quality of work is being perceived.

☐ 8. Learning to do professional performance appraisals is excellent preparation for advancement and increased responsibility.

Research reflects that more than half the professional and clerical employees working today do not understand how their work is evaluated. If this could be true of your employees, familiarize them with the process now and tell every new employee how they will be evaluated when they begin work.

Performance appraisal discussions are normally initiated by the supervisor, but are also appropriate when employees request a meeting to determine how well you think they are doing.

OPPORTUNITIES FOR APPRAISAL DISCUSSION

OPPORTUNITIES FOR PERFORMANCE APPRAISALS

Check ☑ those that apply to you.

☐ 1. Appraisal discussions should be scheduled on a regular basis by either organizational policy or the supervisor.

☐ 2. Less formal discussions may be conducted whenever the nature of the assignment or other circumstances make it meaningful to do so.

☐ 3. Leaders should provide praise for achievement whenever appropriate, and take prompt action to correct unsatisfactory performance when it occurs.

☐ 4. Appraisal activities handled at a propitious moment may be recalled later during a more formal, scheduled review for reinforcement.

☐ 5. Follow-up discussions after a formal appraisal provide the opportunity for a broader review if needed.

PART

II

SETTING
THE STAGE

ESTABLISHING THE RIGHT CLIMATE

Performance appraisal has never been easy for managers or employees. Under the best of circumstances and in a reasonable business environment, performance appraisal requires sensitive attention to the needs of people, responsible concern for productivity and open communication about the expectations of the organization. In an era of rapid change, the process becomes even more complex.

Warren Bennis, co-author of ''LEADERS,'' was asked following a speech to describe the current management scene. He said, ''It is the most difficult, treacherous, blind time in history.'' No one in his audience disagreed.

Managers have been caught in a whirlpool of change which has often diminished their financial resources, reduced their staff, cut their training budget and increased their personal workload. They have witnessed, and often presided over, the elimination of layers of management and support staff which included many friends and trusted associates.

Conditions at home, in the community and throughout the world are also changing rapidly. Working couples are stressed by the need for child care, the pursuit of dual careers, conflicting goals and changing roles in the home. On the national front, major concerns include a deteriorating educational system, the national debt, poverty, crime and continuing issues pertaining to race and sexual preferences. People are staggered by the complexity of the problems and long for answers and anchors in their life at home and at work.

Organizations, while contributing to some of these distractions, need the full focus of their managers and employees on productivity, profitability and customer satisfaction more than ever to be successful in a global economy. Managers, as always, are expected to overcome the obstacles and solve the problems.

> THE ART OF PROGRESS IS TO PRESERVE ORDER AMID CHANGE AND TO PRESERVE CHANGE AMID ORDER.
> —Alfred North Whitehead

ARE YOU PART OF THE SOLUTION, OR PART OF THE PROBLEM?

> Streamlined bureaucracies may translate into higher profits, more responsive customer service and faster product development, but they are also forcing difficult adjustments in how managers work. Many managers must adapt to fuzzier lines of authority and greater emphasis on teamwork.
>
> Low level managers, accustomed to carrying out orders, suddenly are asked to set strategy. For most, a leaner structure means not only increased work loads, but diminished chances for promotion, and the frustration that fosters.
>
> —Carol Hymowitz

To set a climate for effective performance appraisals today, the manager has to work harder than ever before to provide a working environment in which employees can find definitions of their work, the organization's goals, a future they can believe in and meaning for their own career. Before managers can do this for employees, however, they must first do it for themselves.

Review the checklist on the following page and summarize your situation at the present time.

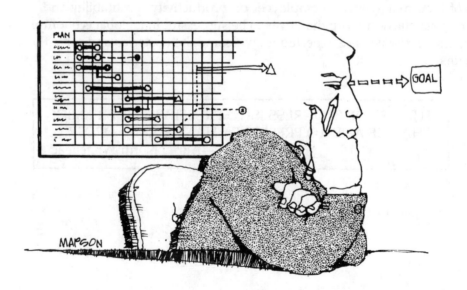

TEST YOUR REALITIES

Whether you have experienced major change in your organization and assignment or not, it pays to periodically ask yourself, ''Why am I here?'', ''What am I supposed to do?'', and ''How well am I doing it?'' In the list below, check your current realities.

_____ 1. I am busier than ever before.

_____ 2. My vision of the future is fuzzy and I am not sure where to focus.

_____ 3. Employees are upset, confused and demoralized.

_____ 4. Expectations of me exceed my ability to produce.

_____ 5. I am understaffed.

_____ 6. I have to delegate to people I feel are not ready.

_____ 7. Resources to reward good work are very limited.

_____ 8. Employees spend more time worrying than working.

_____ 9. I don't know how much longer my job will last.

_____ 10. The actions of the organization are increasingly difficult to support.

_____ 11. My relationships with people are growing weaker.

_____ 12. I never felt better in my life.

_____ 13. I know exactly where the organization is going.

_____ 14. Organizational priorities are clear to me.

_____ 15. Expectations of employees are easy to define.

_____ 16. It is easy to keep employees focused.

_____ 17. Leading and motivating employees is not a problem.

_____ 18. Career opportunities for employees are plentiful.

_____ 19. Advancement opportunities for me are evident.

_____ 20. Morale continues to improve.

_____ 21. Resources are available to properly reward good work.

_____ 22. Performance appraisal usually goes smoothly.

If you checked any of the first eleven items, it is strongly suggested you do some serious analysis of your current realities and the climate for performance appraisal in your organization. The following pages should be helpful.

GET YOUR ACT TOGETHER

Managers who are uncertain about an organization's vision of the future, and are tentative in terms of their own personal commitment to what they perceive as its primary goals, will not do an adequate job themselves (much less favorably influence the work of others). Regardless of how this condition comes about, there are two basic ways to take corrective action. One is to get your act together and the other is to leave the organization. Those who wish to first try getting their act together will find the following suggestions helpful.

1. If you are in an organization in transition, it will help you to clarify issues if you list what you have lost, what has stayed the same and what you have gained.

   LOST _____

   _____

   STAYED THE SAME _____

   _____

   _____

   GAINED _____

   _____

   _____

2. Identify exactly what it is that is bothering you. (Summarize below or take a sheet of paper and write it out in detail.)

   _____

   _____

   _____

   _____

   _____

MANAGERS WHO ARE NOT COMMITTED TO THE GOALS OF THEIR ORGANIZATION WILL NOT BE HELPFUL TO EMPLOYEES OR EFFECTIVE APPRAISERS OF PEFORMANCE.

3. List the issues, obstacles or people preventing you from making a strong commitment, establishing goals and developing expectations with your employees.

ISSUES   OBSTACLES   PEOPLE

_____   _____   _____

_____   _____   _____

_____   _____   _____

4. Describe your attitude and its likely impact on others with whom you work.

_____

_____

_____

5. Share your concerns with persons who can do something about them. List their names below.

_____   _____

_____   _____

_____   _____

6. Identify the contributions your unit can make to the organization.

_____

_____

_____

_____

7. List six actions you will take to help your group make the contributions you have identified.

(1) _____ (4) _____

(2) _____ (5) _____

(3) _____ (6) _____

> A ROCK PILE CEASES TO BE A ROCK PILE THE MOMENT A SINGLE MAN CONTEMPLATES IT, BEARING WITHIN HIM THE IMAGE OF A CATHEDRAL.
> —Antoine de Saint-Exupery

HELP EMPLOYEES FIND MEANING IN THEIR JOBS AND STAY ON COURSE.

> Example is not the main thing in influencing others. It's the only thing.
> —Albert Schweitzer

If you sometimes find it difficult to understand and commit to the current and future needs of your organization, isn't it likely your employees have similar problems? Doesn't it seem logical that they need your leadership to help them understand the issues and to focus their effort in the right places? When you have your act together, you can help employees do the same. Your efforts, and theirs, will create a climate in which performance appraisal is meaningful and mutually supportive. Here are some tips on how to make it happen successfully. Check those you are now using or will use in the future.

_____ 1. Reflect a positive, "can and will do" attitude.

_____ 2. Demonstrate personal flexibility and adaptability.

_____ 3. Communicate your vision of the future and how it is bridged to the present.

_____ 4. Identify and talk through the concerns of each individual.

_____ 5. Discuss and clarify organizational, personal and employee objectives. Reduce ambiguity.

_____ 6. Help employees assess their current role, express your expectations and develop a plan to meet job requirements together.

_____ 7. Detemine what employees consider to be problems and involve them in finding solutions.

_____ 8. Fix those things that are broken quickly.

_____ 9. Show employees the importance of turning loose of the past, focusing on the present and anticipating change in the future.

_____ 10. Help employees determine how their personal career goals can be achieved or made more realistic.

_____ 11. Encourage employees to show some initiative and to risk a little. They will grow in the process.

_____ 12. Use delegation to educate and develop people.

_____ 13. Devote whatever resources you have available to recognize and reward desired performance.

_____ 14. Recognize genuine attempts to achieve as well as the achievements themselves.

_____ 15. Make sure policies and procedures always support and never prevent the accomplishment of objectives.

_____ 16. Ask your employees frequently what you and/or the organization are doing that makes them uncomfortable and inhibits their performance.

_____ 17. Be sure your behavior and communication practices continue to be consistent and congruent with what you expect from others.

_____ 18. If your organization is in transition, discuss the emotional impacts with employees so they will understand what they are experiencing is normal. Do help them move on to a new commitment as soon as possible.

PERFORMANCE APPRAISAL SHOULD MAKE EVERY EMPLOYEE AWARE OF THE IMPORTANCE OF THE CONTRIBUTION THEY ARE EXPECTED TO MAKE.

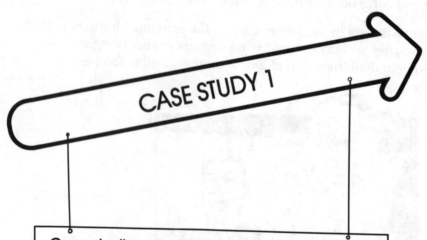

CASE STUDY 1

Case studies provide insights about the content that has been, or is about to be, presented.

The first case (on the facing page) will help you understand some of the ground work necessary to achieve a successful performance appraisal.

WHO WILL BE THE BEST AT PERFORMANCE APPRAISALS?

Case Study #1

Janice and Fletcher are new supervisors attending their first training workshop. They have not covered material on performance appraisals yet, but are discussing their personal philosophies about them over lunch. Janice doesn't believe a fair performance appraisal can be made of an employee's work unless assignments have been discussed, and expectations agreed upon in advance. She thinks work should be assigned in measurable terms so both she and the employee can track performance as the work progresses.

Fletcher thinks this approach is dangerous. He feels employees should be given only a general idea of what is to be accomplished. He thinks employees who participate in establishing performance objectives will set them too low. He prefers to leave performance expectations vague to see what the employees accomplish on their own. If their standards don't measure up, he will let them know then and there.

Who do you think will be the best at performance appraisals?

☐ Janice
Because _____

_____

☐ Fletcher
Because _____

_____

Turn to page 78 for the author's views.

PART

III

HOW TO PREPARE FOR MORE EFFECTIVE APPRAISALS

WHAT IS MEANT BY GOALS AND STANDARDS?

The appraisal process starts when the employee and supervisor reach a mutual understanding of what needs to be accomplished. If expectations are not clearly stated, mutually understood and presented in measurable terms, performance will be difficult to evaluate.

Goals and standards are methods by which job expectations can be expressed. Those responsible for performance appraisals need a good understanding of goals and standards, and how to use them during the appraisal process.

See if you agree with the definitions and examples below. Check ☑ the appropriate boxes.

GOALS

☐ A **goal** is a statement of results which are to be achieved. Goals describe: (1) conditions that will exist when the desired outcome has been accomplished; (2) a time frame during which the outcome is to be completed; and (3) resources the organization is willing to commit to achieve the desired result.

Goals should be challenging, but achievable and established with the participation of those responsible for meeting them. Here is an example:

"To increase the flow of invoices through the Accounting Department to a minimum of 150 per day by October 1. The total cost increase to accomplish this should not exceed $550."

Once accomplished, a new goal can be established to emphasize the next set of desired results.

STANDARDS

☐ A **standard** refers to an ongoing performance criteria that must be met time and time again. Standards are usually expressed quantitatively, and refer to such things as attendance, breakage, manufacturing tolerances, production rates and safety standards. They are the most effective when established with the participation of those who must meet them. Here is an example:

"The departmental filing backlog should not exceed one week. Any record requested should be available within five minutes of the request."

In general, goals apply more to managers and professional employees who engage in individualized projects. Standards are more common for workers engaged in routine, repetitive tasks.

When employees participate in setting goals and standards, there should be no mystery about how their performance will be judged. Employees cannot say, "Why didn't you tell me that's what you wanted?" or, "Who dreamed up these impossible standards?"

Since goals and/or standards are the primary criteria by which performance will be measured, it is worth reviewing them. Please complete the exercise on the facing page.

IDENTIFYING GOALS AND STANDARDS

In the following list of statements, place a ⬛G if it is a goal and an ⬛S in the box if it is a standard according to the definitions on page 25. If the statement is neither a goal nor a standard, leave the ☐ blank. Answers are at the bottom of the page.

☐ 1. Breakage in the kitchen should be kept to a minimum.

☐ 2. To eliminate maintenance coding errors for existing computer programs by October 1, at a cost not to exceed 40 work hours.

☐ 3. Reduce the cost of ongoing operations by January 1.

☐ 4. Telephones are to be answered quickly and messages taken when necessary.

☐ 5. To reduce burner maintenance expense by 15% before November 15, at a one time cost not to exceed $10,000.

☐ 6. To increase sales of men's watches by 10% before June 1, with no increase in expense.

☐ 7. Reduce lost time because of accidents appreciably by year end.

☐ 8. Errors in recording class enrollment will not exceed 2% of the total monthly enrollment.

☐ 9. Telephones should be answered after no more than two rings. Telephone manners are expected to follow that prescribed in the company handbook. Messages should include date, time of call, relevant names and numbers, and the nature of the call.

☐ 10. To increase Western Region sales by $200,000, by year end at an increased cost of sales of less than 5%.

ANSWERS:
Items 2, 5, 6 and 10 are measurable goals.
Items 8 and 9 are measurable standards.
Items 1, 3, 4 and 7 are neither goals nor standards.

OUR ATTITUDE TOWARD PEOPLE
DETERMINES OUR APPROACH TO
PERFORMANCE APPRAISALS

Some leaders do performance appraisals
well because their attitude toward people
set them on a positive course. Others are
less successful because their attitude
creates a negative climate. The next page
describes 3 different attitudes. Which one
best describes you?

ATTITUDES AND PERFORMANCE APPRAISALS

| CHECK ☑ THE ONE THAT BEST DESCRIBES YOU. |

☐ **"I know best."**—This person feels work should be done by controlling the people who do it. Workers are told what to do, how to do it, and when to stop. Then they are told what they did wrong and what they did right; where they are weak, and where they are strong. The person in charge feels this is justified because of his or her superior knowledge and ability. This attitude does not invite new ideas or challenge people. Communication is directed one way only.

☐ **"I'll set the goals, you meet them."**—This person feels that because of superior knowledge, ability or experience, it is O.K. to set goals for others to meet. The worker is given an opportunity to discuss ways to meet goals, but has no input into the actual performance objectives. Performance is evaluated on how well original goals were achieved, regardless of how realistic they were.

☐ **"Let's review the work together, establish some realistic goals and evaluate performance accordingly."**—This person emphasizes work performance, not worker characteristics. The idea is to help workers evaluate the usefulness of their ideas; recognize their weaknesses; and exploit their strengths. The leader acts as a resource and enabler, rather than as a judge.

SELF-ANALYSIS

CHARACTERISTICS OF AN EFFECTIVE APPRAISER

Personal characteristics influence how we do as appraisers. Now is a good time to evaluate your appraisal skills. Complete the assessment on the facing page.

Commit now to improving your skills in any area indicated by your ratings.

CHARACTERISTICS OF AN EFFECTIVE APPRAISER

The following personal characteristics support effective performance appraisals. This scale will help identify your strengths, and determine areas where improvement would be beneficial. Circle the number that best reflects where you fall on the scale. The higher the number, the more the characteristic describes you. When you have finished, total the numbers circled in the space provided.

1.	I like being responsible for productivity.	10 9 8 7 6 5 4 3 2 1
2.	I like people, and enjoy talking with them.	10 9 8 7 6 5 4 3 2 1
3.	I don't mind giving criticism of a constructive nature.	10 9 8 7 6 5 4 3 2 1
4.	I give praise freely when it is earned.	10 9 8 7 6 5 4 3 2 1
5.	I am not intimidated by workers who tell me what they really think.	10 9 8 7 6 5 4 3 2 1
6.	I seek new ideas and use them whenever possible.	10 9 8 7 6 5 4 3 2 1
7.	I respect the knowledge and skill of the people who work for me.	10 9 8 7 6 5 4 3 2 1
8.	I follow up to be sure commitments, goals and standards are being met.	10 9 8 7 6 5 4 3 2 1
9.	I am sensitive to the needs and feelings of others.	10 9 8 7 6 5 4 3 2 1
10.	I am not worried by employees who know more about their work than I do.	10 9 8 7 6 5 4 3 2 1

TOTAL _____.

A score between 90 and 100 indicates you have excellent characteristics to conduct effective appraisals. A score between 70 and 89 indicates that you have significant strengths, but also some improvement needs. Scores between 50 and 69 reflect a significant number of problem areas. Scores below 50 call for a serious effort to improve. Make a special effort to grow in any area where you scored 6 or less, regardless of your total score.

32

CHARACTERISTICS OF AN
EFFECTIVE APPRAISER

LEADING A PERFORMANCE APPRAISAL
DISCUSSION CAN BE COMPARED TO
BASEBALL

(You don't have to be a fan to make it work.)

–Every session requires a team effort and a
game plan.

–Winning depends on how well the team
has prepared.

–Each player needs a turn at bat.

–Four basic essentials (bases) need to be
covered in each meeting to achieve
maximum results.

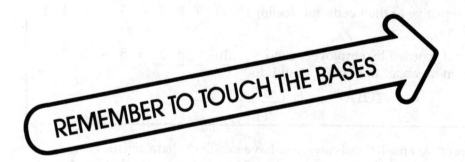

REMEMBER TO TOUCH THE BASES

COVER ALL THE BASES

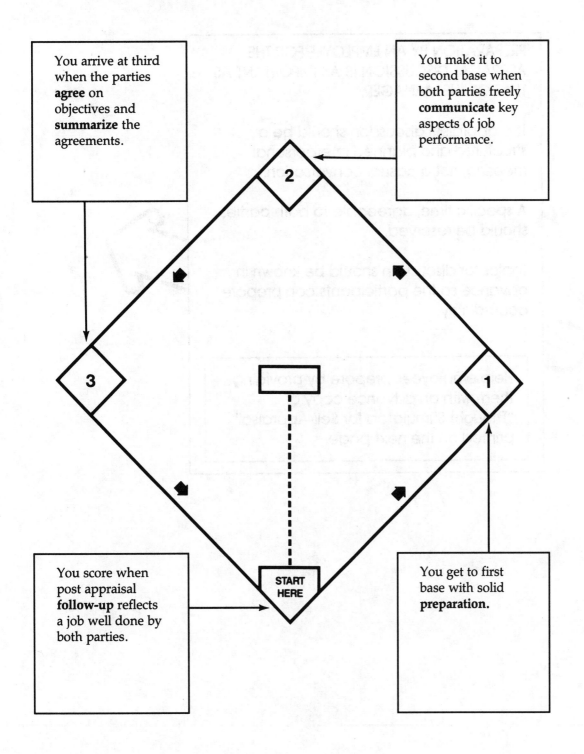

You arrive at third when the parties **agree** on objectives and **summarize** the agreements.

You make it to second base when both parties freely **communicate** key aspects of job performance.

You score when post appraisal **follow-up** reflects a job well done by both parties.

You get to first base with solid **preparation.**

PREPARATION BY AN EMPLOYEE FOR THE APPRAISAL DISCUSSION IS AS IMPORTANT AS THAT OF THE MANAGER.

The appraisal discussion should be a structured and planned interpersonal meeting, not a casual conversation.

A specific time, agreeable to both parties should be reserved.

Topics for discussion should be known in advance so the participants can prepare accordingly.

Help employees prepare by providing them with an advance copy of "Thought Stimulators for Self-Appraisal" printed on the next page.

THOUGHT STIMULATORS FOR SELF-APPRAISAL

These questions can help you prepare for your performance appraisal. As you read each question, think about your performance, your progress, and your plans for future growth.

1. What critical abilities does my job require? To what extent do I fulfill them?

2. What do I like best about my job? Least?

3. What were my specific accomplishments during this appraisal period?

4. Which goals or standards did I fall short of meeting?

5. How could my supervisor help me do a better job?

6. Is there anything that the organization or my supervisor does that hinders my effectiveness?

7. What changes would improve my performance?

8. Does my present job make the best use of my capabilities? How could I become more productive?

9. What do I expect to be doing five years from now?

10. Do I need more experience or training in any aspect of my current job? How could it be accomplished?

11. What have I done since my last appraisal to prepare myself for more responsibility?

12. What new goals and standards should be established for the next appraisal period? Which old ones need to be modified or deleted?

> YOU HAVE PERMISSION TO COPY THIS SHEET FOR
> YOUR EMPLOYEES

A TIP ON HOW TO GET
TO FIRST BASE:

THOROUGH PREPARATION BY THE MANAGER!

WHEN A PERFORMANCE APPRAISAL GOES
POORLY, IT IS USUALLY BECAUSE THE
SUPERVISOR HAS NOT PREPARED PROPERLY
OR COMPLETELY, OR HAS NOT GIVEN THE
EMPLOYEE THE OPPORTUNITY TO PREPARE.

BE PREPARED

MANAGERIAL PREPARATION FOR PLANNING THE APPRAISAL

Prior to conducting a performance appraisal, identify and develop items to be covered. Since employee performance in the current job is the central issue, gather relevant data concerning job requirements and the established goals or standards. Next, assess the employee's performance on the above for the appraisal period. Then:

1. Review the job requirements to be sure you are fully conversant with them.

2. Review the goals and standards you previously discussed and agreed upon with the employee, (plus any notes you have relating to their achievement).

3. Review the employee's history, including:
   — job skills
   — training
   — experience
   — special or unique qualifications
   — past jobs and job performance

4. Evaluate job performance versus job expectations for the period being appraised, and rate it from unacceptable to outstanding.

5. Note any variances in the employee's performance that need to be discussed. Provide specific examples.

6. Consider career opportunities or limitations for this person. Be prepared to discuss them.

WATCH OUT FOR PITFALLS
AS YOU PREPARE!

PITFALLS TO AVOID

Factors that mislead or blind us when we are in the appraisal process are pitfalls to be avoided. An appraiser must be on guard against anything that distorts reality; favorably or unfavorably. Some typical pitfalls include:

— Bias/Prejudice. Things we tend to react to that have nothing to do with performance such as: race, religion, education, family background, age and/or sex.

— Trait Assessment. Too much attention to characteristics that have nothing to do with the job and are difficult to measure. Examples include characteristics such as flexibility, sincerity, or friendliness.

— Over-emphasis on favorable or unfavorable performance of one or two tasks which could lead to an unbalanced evaluation of the overall contribution.

— Relying on impressions rather than facts.

— Holding the employee responsible for the impact of factors beyond his/her control.

— Failure to provide each employee with an opportunity for advance preparation.

CONCENTRATE ON PERFORMANCE MEASURED
AGAINST MUTUALLY UNDERSTOOD EXPECTATIONS.

In an appraisal discussion, four fundamental areas need to be covered:

1. The measurement of results of the employee's performance against goals and/or standards.

2. Recognition of the employee's contributions.

3. Correction of any new or ongoing performance problems.

4. The establishment of goals and or standards for the next appraisal period.

Everything of substance during the discussion should relate to these elements, and both parties should actively participate in the discussion. A plan, prepared in advance, will help keep the discussion on target.

DEVELOP

AN ACTION PLAN

FOR THE DISCUSSION

HERE'S HOW

HOW TO DEVELOP AN ACTION PLAN

Once you have completed your planning review, you will need to develop an action plan for the appraisal. Keep the following guidelines in mind and check ☑ those you expect to use in your action plan.

☐ 1. Don't cover too many areas in any one discussion. Concentrate on those which deserve the most attention.

☐ 2. Make sure there are specific, unbiased examples that can be used to support your points but that also allow for dialogue.

☐ 3. Develop positive approaches to correcting problems. Give the employee an opportunity to suggest solutions before any final decisions are made.

☐ 4. Be prepared to provide praise and positive reinforcement for items which deserve it.

☐ 5. Identify developmental activities that will improve the employee's performance in the present assignment, and/or provide preparation for future assignments.

☐ 6. Note any projects, goals and/or standards to be accomplished during the forthcoming appraisal period. Discuss them and reach agreement on them during the session.

☐ 7. Plan to involve the employee in all aspects of the discussion.

APPRAISAL MODELS

OUTSTANDING? SATISFACTORY?

UNSATISFACTORY?

Your conclusions from the evaluation should be a primary guide to structure the appraisal discussion. Read on for some suggested approaches.

HAVE YOUR DISCUSSION
OBJECTIVES WELL IN MIND AS
YOU PREPARE.

APPRAISAL DISCUSSION MODELS

Your overall evaluation of an employee will range from outstanding to unsatisfactory. Select an approach to your appraisal discussion that is in keeping with your evaluation. The employee, for example, may be outstanding in the current assignment, but not promotable because certain key skills are lacking. You have to decide how to handle each case. Following are some possible discussion models.

END RESULT OF EVALUATION	EMPLOYEE'S LIKELY FUTURE	DISCUSSION OBJECTIVE
Outstanding	Promotion	Consider opportunities
	Growth in present assignment	Make development plans
	Broadened Assignment	Review possibility of extending responsibility
	No change in duties	How to maintain performance level
Satisfactory	Promotion	Consider possibilities
	Growth in present assignment	Make development plans
	No change in duties	How to maintain or improve performance level
Unsatisfactory	Performance correctible	Plan correction and gain commitment
	Performance uncorrectible	Review possible re-assignment, or prepare for termination

NOW IS A GOOD TIME TO APPLY WHAT YOU HAVE READ. ANALYZE THE CASE STUDY ON THE NEXT PAGE BASED ON WHAT YOU HAVE LEARNED.

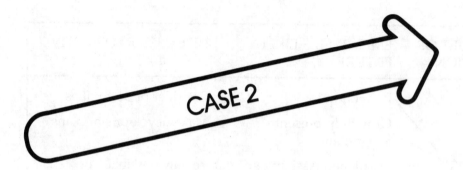

CASE 2

WHAT UPSET JESS?

Case Study #2

Darcy just completed a performance appraisal discussion with one of her employees and is upset about it. She told another supervisor at lunch, "I appraised Jess this morning. I had to call him out of the budget meeting because I remembered all my appraisals were due today. I couldn't believe his reaction. He said he had no time to prepare, and expected me to have an example to support each criticism I made. About all he did, really, was to criticize my position on a couple of issues. I told him several things I didn't like about his performance, and then was good enough to tell him how to correct his faults. All I got back was anger and silence. You would think he would be grateful for some feedback, but I guess people today don't really care about improving. Normally he's a pretty good employee, but he was sure upset during the appraisal. What do you suppose is wrong with him anyway?"

Please use the space below to write down what you think is "wrong" with Jess. Check your answer with the author's on page 78.

_____

_____

_____

_____

_____

_____

_____

_____

_____

PART

IV

CONDUCTING
THE APPRAISAL

PART

IX

CONDUCTING THE APPRAISAL

HOW TO BEGIN THE APPRAISAL DISCUSSION

Managers have the responsibility to initiate appraisal discussions. Although individual personalities will influence the format, experts agree the discussion should be held in a private place to avoid interruptions and should begin on a positive and friendly note. While chit-chat will help break the ice, both parties will welcome getting down to business.

One way to accomplish this is to highlight a specific positive achievement and discuss it first. Another approach is to ask the employee to review his or her accomplishments for the appraisal period. This allows the employee to select where to begin and can lead to a candid assessment of actual performance. While the employee is talking, the leader should be an interested listener.

If variances between expectations and results are evident, it is important both leader and employee try to determine what they are and why they occurred. This helps the discussion become a joint problem-solving session which can lead to the implementation of effective solutions.

The employee should be encouraged to identify as many reasons for variances as possible. None should be rejected right away, even if they seem to be excuses. The leader should also contribute possible causes so nothing significant is overlooked. This sharing allows for an exchange of viewpoints. This can provide better insights for all concerned and lead to a new understanding of the expectations of the organization, and the people who staff it.

THE LEADER MUST BE SURE UNSATISFACTORY PERFORMANCE IS IDENTIFIED AND DISCUSSED.

Experts believe that at least 50% of performance problems in business occur because of a lack of feedback. An employee will see no reason to change performance if it appears acceptable to the supervisor and organization.

Following are some ways to approach constructive feedback, and maintain a climate conducive to a win/win outcome.

NEVER IGNORE UNSATISFACTORY PERFORMANCE!

YOU MAKE IT TO SECOND BASE WHEN BOTH PARTIES FREELY COMMUNICATE ALL ASPECTS OF THE JOB. IT'S NOT AS EASY AS IT SOUNDS!

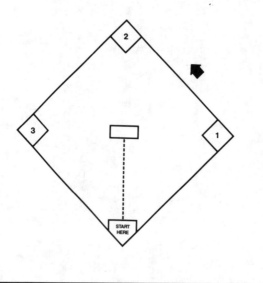

DISCUSSING UNSATISFACTORY PERFORMANCE

Employees who work in a nonthreatening atmosphere are more likely to discuss their shortcomings in the appraisal setting. When this occurs, the supervisor can be supportive by saying something like, "That's very perceptive. What can we do to correct this situation?"

If the employee has been unsatisfactory in an aspect of his or her job, and does not bring up areas of weak performance, the supervisor must do so. It helps to be able to describe the impact of the poor performance on the organization.

Some employees may not realize they are falling short of expectations. Or they may assume everything is acceptable because no one has ever discussed the problem with them. Sometimes they may feel everything is O.K. because they see others doing the same thing.

A first step to correct unsatisfactory performance is to review expectations. If the employee is unaware of these expectations, they must be made clear, and a commitment made that they will be met. If expectations are not being met for some other reason, the supervisor must first learn why, and then agree on a corrective action plan worked out with the employee.

Questions like these can be helpful in opening up the issues:

"Are you aware of the standards for quantity and quality we expect on this item?"

"Are you aware of your error rate versus the departmental average?"

"We seem to be running about two weeks behind schedule; can you tell me why, and what we can do to catch up?"

"Your sales reports are excellent but they are never on time. Can you explain why?"

"Fifty percent of your staff resigned in the last quarter. To what do you attribute that?"

SUCCESSFUL DISCUSSION LEADERS BELIEVE EMPLOYEES SHOULD DO MOST OF THE TALKING. THIS CAN BE ACHIEVED BY USING GOOD COMMUNICATION SKILLS, AND AN ATMOSPHERE THAT ENCOURAGES DISCUSSION.

WAYS TO GET AN EMPLOYEE
TO TALK

HOW TO GET AN EMPLOYEE TO TALK FREELY

Employees often say very little during an appraisal discussion. There are several possible reasons for this. Some include:

— The employee does not understand the purpose of the appraisal, and is afraid to express an opinion.

— The employee is not given the opportunity to express an opinion.

— The employee was not given time to prepare for the discussion.

— The employee's thoughts and ideas are quickly brushed aside or discounted.

— The employee feels the whole process is meaningless.

A manager can overcome this reluctance to enter into a dialogue by creating the right type of nonthreatening atmosphere. Check ☑ those methods you expect to use.

☐ 1. **BE DESCRIPTIVE RATHER THAN JUDGMENTAL.** When a supervisor is judgmental about an employee's performance, it almost always brings out defensive behavior. A better climate is established when descriptive terms are used to describe problems. This makes it possible for the leader and employee to unemotionally discuss a solution, or even better, a solution generated by the employee. Note the differences in the following example:

JUDGMENTAL	DESCRIPTIVE
"How could you do such a dumb thing?"	"Can you explain what caused the incident?"

Leaders who use descriptive, nonjudgmental language in the appraisal discussion show a desire to analyze and resolve a problem, not find a scapegoat or way to demean the employee.

☐ 2. **BE SUPPORTIVE, NOT AUTHORITARIAN.** Supervisors sometimes purposely, and sometimes inadvertently, display an authoritarian attitude during the discussion. This can create resentment and defensiveness. It is usually better to respect the employee's ability to contribute to the solution of a problem. Here is an example.

AUTHORITARIAN	SUPPORTIVE
"Here is what we will do to get this done on time."	"What do you suggest we do to get this done on time in the future?"

Supportive practices generate options for problem solving because the employee is encouraged to make suggestions. They also focus on the problem, not the employee. In addition, a supportive approach promotes better listening by both parties, and permits a climate where disagreement is not only acceptable, but invited.

☐ 3. **REFLECT EQUALITY, NOT SUPERIORITY.** Supervisors who put too much emphasis on their position and power often create barriers between themselves and their employees. Supervisors who share information with employees and then seek their opinions provide a flavor of equality. Here is an example:

SUPERIORITY	EQUALITY
"I was doing it this way before you were born."	"We have done it this way for years but I would like to hear your ideas on how we can do it better."

Employees appreciate a leader who shares information, asks for opinions and listens to ideas. Leaders who understand this have appraisal discussions that are more enlightening and productive.

☐ 4. **BE ACCEPTING, NOT DOGMATIC.** Supervisors who approach decisions, plans and problems dogmatically are telling employees there is no need for other ideas or solutions. Things have already been decided. This can demoralize an employee who has ideas and wants to excel. Leaders who listen to employee input, or allow their ideas to be challenged in a search for the best solution, stimulate enthusiasm, creativity and productivity. Here is an example that contrasts the two approaches:

DOGMATIC	ACCEPTING
"This is the best solution."	This is the best solution I could come up with. What other possibilities do you see?"

A supervisor who accepts employee's input recognizes their value, capitalizes on their knowledge and builds confidence in the group.

> SUPERVISORS LEARN MORE
> FROM LISTENING THAN
> TALKING!

THOUGHTFUL QUESTIONS CAN PROVIDE SOME
VERY IMPORTANT SIDE BENEFITS, BECAUSE:

- They require the leader's commitment to
  listen.

- They stimulate thought about specific
  issues.

- They solicit another person's ideas, point
  of view or feelings.

- They provide an opportunity to test an
  idea against the reasoning of someone
  else.

- They elicit important information that
  might not otherwise be available.

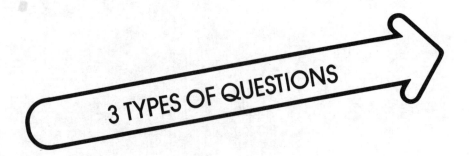

3 TYPES OF QUESTIONS

QUESTIONS THAT FACILITATE APPRAISAL DISCUSSIONS

There are three types of questions that can be used to help the supervisor and employee better understand each other's point of view. Check ☑ those you would feel comfortable using.

☐ 1. <u>OPEN QUESTIONS</u>—Questions which cannot be answered with a yes or no. These questions require an opinion or expression of feelings. For example: ''What is your opinion of...?'' ''How do you feel about...?'' ''What do you think caused....?''

> Advantages of open questions include:
>
> — a demonstration of your interest in the other person's point of view;
>
> — a confirmation that you value the other person's ideas and feelings;
>
> — a stimulation of thought about specific issues;
>
> — a better understanding of the other person's needs;
>
> — the encouragement of a dialogue rather than a monologue.

☐ 2. **REFLECTIVE QUESTIONS**—A reflective question repeats a statement the other person has made in the form of a question. Good listening skills are required. It is also important to select the most significant feeling or idea stated. For example:

> *Employee: "Our results would be better if we modified the procedures used to take samples."*

> *Supervisor: "You're convinced the results can be improved?"*

Reflective questions can be helpful because:

— arguments can be avoided. You respond without accepting or rejecting what has been said.

— it confirms you understand what has been said. If you reflect incorrectly, the other party has an opportunity to correct you.

— the other person is encouraged to clarify or expand upon what has been said.

— the other person can recognize illogical statements they may have made if the statement comes back in a nondirective fashion.

— they create a dialogue conducive for agreement.

☐ 3. **<u>DIRECTIVE QUESTIONS</u>**—These are used to solicit information about a particular point or issue. Directive questions are usually reserved until after the other person has finished talking on the subject. Directive questions can then be used to sustain communication, or obtain information or ideas in which you are specifically interested. Here is an example:

Supervisor—''If you are convinced the results can be improved, what steps would you take and when would you take them?''

Directive questions have these advantages:

— They provide pertinent information in those areas of greatest importance to you.

— They challenge the other person to explore ideas, defend statements, and contribute suggestions.

— They offer both parties specific facts on an issue.

Open, reflective and **directive** questions are all useful techniques to draw the employee into a thorough discussion of job performance and personal development.

The appraisal discussion is more than a simple review of job performance. It should progress naturally to a discussion of how the employee can do a better job in the future.

It is also a good time to draw out the employee's ambitions and aspirations.

PERSONAL DEVELOPMENT AND GROWTH

As performance is discussed, it often becomes apparent that additional training and development is required or desirable. It is also possible the discussion will provide an indication that an employee is ready for more responsibility which requires new or improved skills.

Therefore, specific areas for improvement and the need for new skill development should be discussed. Techniques by which further growth can be accomplished should also be covered. The leader should encourage the employee to talk about personal growth needs, so goals to meet them can be established. This effort can be supported by:

— Serving as a sounding board to explore developmental alternatives.

— Testing the extent to which the employee has thought through developmental objectives.

— Providing a supportive climate for learning.

The final employee development plans should be specific and include agreement by the employee for:

— What the employee needs to do.

— When the employee needs to do it.

— What the leader needs to do and when.

— Once development is completed, how it is to be applied.

CHARACTERISTICS OF AN EFFECTIVE
DISCUSSION LEADER

The appraiser's attitude toward the appraisal discussion will make a genuine difference in the outcome. A well-led session provides an opportunity to share ideas and points of view, and to discuss problems and successes. Examine your attitude on the next page.

SELF-ANALYSIS

CHARACTERISTICS OF AN EFFECTIVE DISCUSSION LEADER

The following characteristics are essential to effective performance appraisal discussions. This scale will help you identify strengths and determine areas where improvement would be beneficial. Circle the number that best reflects where you fall on the scale. The higher the number, the more you are like the characteristic. When you have finished, total the numbers circled in the space provided.

1.	I let the employee do most of the talking.	10 9 8 7 6 5 4 3 2 1
2.	I make an intense effort to listen to the employee's ideas.	10 9 8 7 6 5 4 3 2 1
3.	I am prepared to suggest solutions to problems and development needs but let the employee contribute first.	10 9 8 7 6 5 4 3 2 1
4.	My statements about performance are descriptive, not judgmental.	10 9 8 7 6 5 4 3 2 1
5.	I reinforce the positives in performance as well as seeking ways to eliminate the negatives.	10 9 8 7 6 5 4 3 2 1
6.	I try to support the employee's ideas rather than force my own.	10 9 8 7 6 5 4 3 2 1
7.	I invite alternatives rather than assume there is only one way to approach an issue.	10 9 8 7 6 5 4 3 2 1
8.	I use open-ended, reflective and directive questions to stimulate discussion.	10 9 8 7 6 5 4 3 2 1
9.	I am specific and descriptive when I express a concern about performance.	10 9 8 7 6 5 4 3 2 1
10.	My employees know I want them to succeed.	10 9 8 7 6 5 4 3 2 1

TOTAL _____.

A score between 90 and 100 indicates you should be leading successful discussions. Scores between 70 and 89 indicate significant strengths plus a few improvement needs. A score between 50 and 69 reflects some strengths, but a significant number of problem areas as well. Scores below 50 call for a serious effort to improve in several categories. Make a special effort to grow in any area where you scored 6 or less regardless of your total score.

YOU ARRIVE AT THIRD BASE WHEN BOTH
PARTIES AGREE ON A PERFORMANCE PLAN
FOR THE NEXT PERIOD AND SUMMARIZE THESE
AGREEMENTS.

2

3

1

START
HERE

WRAPPING IT UP

CLOSING THE APPRAISAL DISCUSSION

When the supervisor and employee have concluded discussion of past performance, addressed any development needs and established new goals and/or standards for the future, they need to take time to review these agreements and plans. Many performance reviews fail because participants end the session with differing perceptions about what was accomplished and what was agreed. To prevent this the leader should conclude the discussion by:

1. Summarizing what has been discussed and agreed. This should be done positively and enthusiastically.

2. Giving the employee a chance to react, question, and add additional ideas and suggestions.

3. Expressing appreciation for the employee's participation and reinforcing the commitment to future plans.

4. Following the discussion with a written record of the agreements and/or required action plans.

EMPLOYEE RESPONSE TO THE
APPRAISAL MAY DIFFER FROM
WHAT YOU EXPECT

It is a good idea therefore to give some
thought to the range of possible
responses in advance, and make plans
accordingly.

How would you respond to the employee
behavior described in the following case
situations?

CASE SITUATIONS

Here are some situations about ways employees responded to their appraisal.
After reading each example, indicate how you would react.

SITUATION 1

The employee agrees with the appraisal and wants to improve. Some genuine
differences of opinion are expressed, but the employee makes positive efforts
to clarify the issues rather than be defensive.

YOUR RESPONSE _____

_____

_____

_____

_____

SITUATION 2

> The employee does not accept responsibility for his substandard performance and blames company politics and other employees.

YOUR RESPONSE _____

_____

_____

_____

SITUATION 3

> The employee disagrees with elements of your appraisal and offers specific information to refute your findings.

YOUR RESPONSE _____

_____

_____

_____

SITUATION 4

> The employee accepts the appraisal without saying a word and prepares to leave before you have discussed the next performance plan.

YOUR RESPONSE _____

_____

_____

_____

Compare your response with the author on page 78 and 79.

P A R T

V

FOLLOWING UP

YOU SCORE WHEN A POST-APPRAISAL ANALYSIS
REFLECTS A JOB WELL DONE BY BOTH PARTIES

FOLLOWING UP— THREE SUGGESTIONS

1 WRITTEN RECORDS

Once the performance appraisal discussion has been concluded, a manager should immediately make a written record of:

— the overall appraisal for the previous period;

— plans which both parties agreed to;

— any personal commitments requiring specific action.

A copy of this summary should be given to the employee.

2 REFLECTION

Following each review is a good time to review your performance in leading the discussion. Some good questions are:

— What was done well?

— What was done poorly?

— What will be done differently next time?

— What was learned about the employee?

— What was learned about self and job?

3 FOLLOW THROUGH

A third element of follow-up is to ensure that agreements are kept and plans followed. If this is not done, the entire appraisal loses its impact and the employee assumes no one cares very much about performance. This phase of the follow-up is actually the initial phase of the next appraisal.

> To review what you have read, and to plan your next performance appraisal, study the check list on the next 2 pages.

A PERFORMANCE APPRAISAL CHECKLIST FOR MANAGERS

The following checklist is designed to guide the manager in preparing, conducting and following through on employee performance appraisal discussions.

I PERSONAL PREPARATION

☐ I have reviewed mutually understood expectations with respect to job duties, projects, goals, standards, and any other pre-determined performance factors pertinent to this appraisal discussion.

☐ I have observed job performance measured against mutually understood expectations. In so doing, I have done my best to avoid such pitfalls as:
_____ Bias/prejudice
_____ The vagaries of memory
_____ Over-attention to some aspects of the job at the expense of others
_____ Being overly influenced by my own experience
_____ Trait evaluation rather than performance measurement

☐ I have reviewed the employee's background including:
_____ Skills
_____ Work experience
_____ Training

☐ I have determined the employee's performance strengths and areas in need of improvement and in so doing have:
_____ Accumulated specific, unbiased documentation that can be used to help communicate my position
_____ Limited myself to those critical points that are the most important
_____ Prepared a possible development plan in case the employee needs assistance in coming up with a suitable plan

☐ I have identified areas for concentration in setting goals and standards for the next appraisal period.

☐ I have given the employee advance notice of when the discussion will be held so that he/she can prepare.

☐ I have set aside an adequate block of uninterrupted time to permit a full and complete discussion.

II CONDUCTING THE APPRAISAL DISCUSSION

☐ I plan to begin the discussion by creating a sincere, but open and friendly atmosphere. This includes:
_____ Reviewing the purpose of the discussion
_____ Making it clear that it is a joint discussion for the purpose of mutual problem solving and goal setting
_____ Striving to put the employee at ease

☐ In the body of the discussion I intend to keep the focus on job performance and related factors. This includes:
_____ Discussing job requirements—employee strengths, accomplishments, improvement needs and evaluating results of performance against objectives set during previous reviews and discussions
_____ Being prepared to cite observations for each point I want to discuss
_____ Encouraging the employee to appraise his/her own performance
_____ Using open, reflective and directive questions to promote thought, understanding and problem solving

☐ I will encourage the employee to outline his/her personal plans for self-development before suggesting ideas of my own. In the process, I will:
_____ Try to get the employee to set personal growth and improvement targets
_____ Strive to reach agreement on appropriate development plans which detail what the employee intends to do, a timetable and support I am prepared to give

☐ I am prepared to discuss work assignments, projects and goals for the next appraisal period and will ask the employee to come prepared with suggestions.

III CLOSING THE DISCUSSION

☐ I will be prepared to make notes during the discussion for the purpose of summarizing agreements and follow up. In closing, I will:
_____ Summarize what has been discussed
_____ Show enthusiasm for plans that have been made
_____ Give the employee an opportunity to make additional suggestions
_____ End on a positive, friendly, harmonious note

IV POST APPRAISAL FOLLOW UP

☐ As soon as the discussion is over, I will record the plans made, points requiring follow up, the commitments I made, and provide a copy for the employee.

☐ I will also evaluate how I handled the discussion.
_____ What I did well
_____ What I could have done better
_____ What I learned about the employee and his/her job
_____ What I learned about myself and my job

REFLECT FOR A MOMENT ON WHAT YOU
HAVE BEEN LEARNING – THEN DEVELOP
AN ACTION PLAN TO APPLY THE CONCEPTS.
THE GUIDE ON THE NEXT PAGE MAY HELP.

Think over the material in this book: the self-analysis
questionnaires, the case studies, and the reinforcement
exercises. What did you learn about performance
appraisals? What did you learn about yourself? How
can you apply what you learned? Make a commitment
to become better at performance appraisals. Design
a personal action plan to help accomplish this goal.

The action plan on the facing page may help clarify
your goals, and outline appropriate action to achieve
those goals.

A PERSONAL ACTION PLAN

1. My appraisal skills are strong in the following areas:

   _____

   _____

   _____

   _____

2. I need to improve the following appraisal skills:

   _____

   _____

   _____

   _____

3. My appraisal improvement goals are: (Be sure they are specific, attainable and measurable.)

   _____

   _____

   _____

   _____

4. Here are my action steps to accomplish my goals.

   _____

   _____

   _____

   _____

   NAME

VOLUNTARY CONTRACT

Sometimes our desire to improve personal skills can be reinforced by making a contract with a friend, spouse, or supervisor. If you believe a contract would help, use the form on the facing page.

CONSIDER A VOLUNTARY CONTRACT

VOLUNTARY
CONTRACT*

I, _____ , hereby agree
(Your name)

to meet with the individual designated below within

thirty days to discuss my progress toward incorporating the

techniques and ideas presented in this program. The purpose

of this meeting will be to *review* areas of strength and

establish action steps for areas where improvement may

still be required.

_____
Signature

I agree to meet with the above individual on

_____
Month   *Date*   *Time*

at the following location.

_____

_____
Signature

*This agreement can be initiated either by you or your
superior. Its purpose is to motivate you to incorporate
concepts and techniques of this program into your
daily activities. It also provides a degree of
accountability between you and your employer.

AUTHOR'S SUGGESTED ANSWERS TO CASES

WHO WILL BE BEST AT PERFORMANCE APPRAISALS?

With proper training and guidance, Janice and Fletcher may both become excellent at performance appraisal. At this point, however, Janice has better instincts about how an appraisal should be approached. Employees need to know what is expected of them. When employees have an opportunity to participate in establishing goals and standards they usually make good contributions. Contrary to Fletcher's assumption, workers tend to set goals and standards too high rather than too low.

WHAT UPSET JESS?

Jess may be upset because Darcy seems to have an attitude that reflects "I know best—what could you possibly contribute to this discussion of your performance?" Jess was asked to leave a meeting to come in for his appraisal discussion. This may have embarassed him. It also suggests that the discussion had not been scheduled in advance, so he had no opportunity to prepare. Darcy's approach seems to be "here's what is wrong and here's what to do about it." Jess has no opportunity for questions or input. How would you react under similar circumstances?

SITUATION 1

Express gratitude for the employee's active participation. This employee has voiced the expected response if you follow the process described in this book. Most employees want information about their strengths and weaknesses, and how to invest their time more profitably for improvement. Don't forget the importance of sincere praise when it is earned.

SITUATION 2

Listen with an open mind. Without interrupting or arguing, try to find out why the person is placing the blame elsewhere. Then move the discussion toward corrective action that can be achieved with the employee's cooperation. Compliment the employee anytime a move is made toward accepting responsibility. Follow up closely and schedule another review soon to measure changes in the employee's point of view.

SITUATION 3

Listen carefully to the employee. Then indicate your willingness to re-examine your data. If it develops that the employee's information is more valid than yours, modify your position accordingly. If you believe the employee's data is invalid, or irrelevant, stand your ground and explain your position.

SITUATION 4

Some individuals are intimidated by the appraisal process and a special effort is required to open things up. Others may feel a quick agreement will save them from a discussion of their faults. When employees are reluctant to talk, encourage them by asking questions. Ask them to suggest activities which would help them. Ask them to summarize their performance. Ask their conclusions at the end of the session. Ensure they provide input about their new performance plan.

NOTES

NOTES

NOTES

NOTES

NOTES

NOTES

NOTES

NOW AVAILABLE FROM CRISP PUBLICATIONS

Books • Videos • CD Roms • Computer-Based Training Products

If you enjoyed this book, we have great news for you. There are over 200 books available in the *50-Minute*™ Series. To request a free full-line catalog, contact your local distributor or Crisp Publications, Inc., 1200 Hamilton Court, Menlo Park, CA 94025. Our toll-free number is 800-442-7477.

Subject Areas Include:

Management

Human Resources

Communication Skills

Personal Development

Marketing/Sales

Organizational Development

Customer Service/Quality

Computer Skills

Small Business and Entrepreneurship

Adult Literacy and Learning

Life Planning and Retirement

CRISP WORLDWIDE DISTRIBUTION

English language books are distributed worldwide. Major international distributors include:

ASIA/PACIFIC

Australia/New Zealand: In Learning, PO Box 1051 Springwood QLD, Brisbane, Australia 4127
Telephone: 7-3841-1061, Facsimile: 7-3841-1580   ATTN: Messrs. Gordon

Singapore: Graham Brash (Pvt) Ltd. 32, Gul Drive, Singapore 2262
Telephone: 65-861-1336, Facsimile: 65-861-4815   ATTN: Mr. Campbell

CANADA

Reid Publishing, Ltd., Box 69559-109 Thomas Street, Oakville, Ontario Canada L6J 7R4.
Telephone: (905) 842-4428, Facsimile: (905) 842-9327   ATTN: Mr. Reid

Trade Book Stores: Raincoast Books, 8680 Cambie Street, Vancouver, British Columbia, Canada V6P 6M9.
Telephone: (604) 323–7100, Facsimile: 604-323-2600   ATTN: Ms. Laidley

EUROPEAN UNION

England: Flex Training, Ltd. 9-15 Hitchin Street, Baldock, Hertfordshire, SG7 6A, England
Telephone: 1-462-896000, Facsimile: 1-462-892417   ATTN: Mr. Willetts

INDIA

Multi-Media HRD, Pvt., Ltd., National House, Tulloch Road, Appolo Bunder, Bombay, India 400-039
Telephone: 91-22-204-2281, Facsimile: 91-22-283-6478   ATTN: Messrs. Aggarwal

MIDDLE EAST

United Arab Emirates: Al-Mutanabbi Bookshop, PO Box 71946, Abu Dhabi
Telephone: 971-2-321-519, Facsimile: 971-2-317-706   ATTN: Mr. Salabbai

SOUTH AMERICA

Mexico: Grupo Editorial Iberoamerica, Serapio Rendon #125, Col. San Rafael, 06470 Mexico, D.F.
Telephone: 525-705-0585, Facsimile: 525-535-2009   ATTN: Señor Grepe

SOUTH AFRICA

Alternative Books, Unit A3 Sanlam Micro Industrial Park, Hammer Avenue STRYDOM Park, Randburg, 2194 South Africa
Telephone: 2711 792 7730, Facsimile: 2711 792 7787   ATTN: Mr. de Haas